Table of Contents

A Mess

Pudgy little toes bend backward at the joints as she kneels on cold, bathroom tile. The floor is slick with oil. It slides and smears and thins but it never goes away. Her pudgy little hands cling desperately to the rag that is meant to soak up the stain, but the oil just spreads. She doesn't understand. She hasn't been taught yet. I haven't taught her yet. She looks up at me, Mommy, I'm trying to clean it up. I'm trying to clean it up, I swear. *The floor will always smell of newborns, of beginnings and birth; the rag will bear the stains of my daughter's efforts like a memoir. Still, the oil will remain. Sweet girl, she doesn't understand.*

I dreamt of being an author. I dreamt of my words on crisp, cream paper, but the price is so steep-- there's no way to learn without having experience, no way to learn without a fortune I was not born to possess. I work days and nights, panting like a dog as I crawl into the bank. I pay what I can, but each time I do, my debt only grows. I have sold my life to the university that was meant to provide me a better one.

Pudgy hands cling desperately to the rag that is meant to wash away her mistake, but the oil only spreads. It coats her knees, her legs, her hands like a second skin. It is thin, as invisible as the sheen of sweat on her brow, but it remains. She doesn't know how long it will take to get her clean, but I don't mind. I will wash her skin when she grows tired and desperate for help, if she ever does. My daughter is a stubborn thing. She looks to the shower, perhaps thinking it may cleanse her, but she looks back down; the floor will remain slick with oil. She looks as though she sees no point, she hasn't finished cleaning, so she continues on scrubbing away.

I dreamt of buying a home, but the hill is so steep, I fell before I could take my first step down the side of it. I meant to mind my feet, meant to keep to the side but the rock slid out from under me. I work days and nights, paying my rent only to have it raised a year later. I live in a home that belongs to a company that sees nothing but my address when I request maintenance. I pay the same price whether the dishes are clean, my clothes can be washed, there's water to drink. I live in a home that was never meant to house me. I live in a home that I was not born to own.

Still, I continue on, I never stop working.

Pudgy little fingers swipe oil across the eyes, trapping tears on the skin. She scrubs and scrapes at her face, but the grease remains. I know better than to offer my help. She's been a stubborn little thing since the day she was born, and I know better than to get in her way. Tears flow harder and faster, the night grows longer and lonelier, still the rag goes back and forth. Still the oil remains. I watch her from the sidelines, waiting to offer my help.

I have dreamt of love, of marriage, but the price is so steep. I can barely afford to live, to eat, how could I afford the marital braids? How could I keep the knot from coming undone? I was not born for baby's breath or champagne. I was not born for warm white lights and cathedrals. Still, I dream of love like fire in the winter, as though I can afford to keep it.

Pudgy little fingers rest peacefully beneath the head. She sleeps now, and when she rises, she will clean. She will sleep, she will rise, and she will clean until her skin tears like paper, until her knuckles protrude like notches on a tree branch. She will sleep, she will rise, she will clean, and the oil will remain, always a presence on the skin. I will haunt this doorway, always a presence waiting to hold her, to grab the soap, to exchange her rag for a paper towel.

I will dream for the rest of my life. I will work like a dog, panting all the while, spreading my money over my debt like a salve. But my money will only thin while that stain remains. I'll dream of cars and appliances I will never be able to afford under the thumb of livable wage. I'll dream of a life with children, a husband and dogs that would starve in the class I was born into. I will strain my neck, dreaming of the top of that mountain, while living at the bottom.

Pudgy little hands, cling desperately to the rag. She looks up at me, Mommy, help.

The Visitor

The following is dedicated to Kyshaun Summers

Come over for dinner anytime

Sera did her best to ignore the seven, dusty clocks in Jenkins Manor, suspended yet always ticking in its many dated and lifeless rooms. She'd never wanted to live there. She wanted to travel, perhaps to Italy or Rome. She imagined herself walking down the streets of Vatican City, calling out to vendors and close friends. Yet, this is not a story of expedition or escapade. When her mother passed, she did indeed move back into that old, tired house, and every day after, she tried to ignore the stiffness in her neck as she passed through the halls and the chilled air that plagued the manor year-round.

Sera had spent summers there as a child. Back then, there was an old swing hanging from an oak tree just off the back porch. She'd stay there for hours, until her mother finally called her in for supper or sunscreen. She loved to play in the trees beside the house and ride her bike up and down the driveway; though, she lived so entirely in her imagination that the driveway often became a massive bridge, the trees became soaring towers. Sera never allowed herself to be lucid within the property for very long, and it is because of this, Sera believes, that it had felt so lively, so vivid when she was younger. The house felt like a shadow now, its beauty made visible only by the illumination of memories of the past.

It was quaint, too small to be called a manor. Two stories of deep mahogany wood and red, vintage runners– which had to be stapled to the main staircase just a few short years ago, when the cancer had made it too difficult for Sera's mother to climb the steps. The walls were adorned in arbitrarily placed drapes, gathered and tied to the walls by golden cords. The paintings, and there were many, were plastered to large sheets of glass rather than framed; Sera's mother had not wanted to box in the creativity that flowed through the canvas. She wanted to touch the paint and smell the thread. She'd wanted to experience them, not just observe.

Upon many, mismatched shelves were tiny trinkets, bobbles, and souvenirs from a life well lived. Sera found herself surrounded by the past. Awake or asleep, she felt it sitting on her skin like the thin veil of humidity that hangs in the trees outside the house every winter. Sera's mother had a difficult time parting with anything, especially material items. A thimble, generations old, sat on a shelf near the front door. Taiwanese meditation balls, placed neatly in their box, sat on the table next to the sofa. It was a terribly uncomfortable sofa, but Sera's mother had spent many of her last days on the leftmost cushion, so Sera could never bring herself to throw it away. Often though, Sera found herself forgetting whether or not she had done away with different things. One morning she would wake up and a side table would be missing; another time, she would come home and find the rug in the living room had disappeared. Items of her mother's clothing, furniture from the many guest rooms, would suddenly vanish. *I must've sold that,* she would think to herself.

All in all, Sera thought the house was stuffy. Her mother was *too* present in its walls. Most nights, she found it difficult to sleep. On some of those nights, she would venture down into the kitchen; she would light the stove and warm some milk while gazing out the window above the sink— a window guarded by iron bars, twisted into spirals and leaves. The manor was terribly cold in the winter, so she relished the warmth in her cup as it flowed down her throat and settled into her stomach. On some of those nights, while peering out the window, she would see her mother, beckoning her, standing by the oak tree that supported the swing and shaded the storm cellar. Sera could almost hear her voice as if they were speaking on the phone, could hear her mother saying, *Sera, why aren't you here? Why aren't you here?* Sera didn't know where her mother could possibly want her to go. No, she was already in the house. She was already home. *Yes*, she would think, *I am right where I ought to be. This is nothing but a dream.* Still, she couldn't bring herself to peer at any of the seven clocks in the manor.

It was a rather noisy house. The floors creaked and cringed where you stepped, the door hinges squeaked as they swung open, the pipes would bang inside the walls so long as they didn't freeze—and of course all the clocks chimed on the hour. There were other, more pleasant sounds as well. Birds chirped in the morning, the tea kettle singing along with them, and the leaves on every tree that surrounded the manor would rustle with the wind. Though, above all, the sound of a particular set of knuckles rapping at the front door was Sera's favorite.

"Hi there!" Sera had always liked Jacob. He lived just a few minutes down the street. He'd come over for something– "I was hoping I could borrow your oven." The way he spoke made her chest warm. His face danced with every word; his eyes always alight with fervor. "Mine's just busted, I'm afraid."

"Of course! Yes, please, come in." He was carrying bags, Sera realized. Probably full of whatever food he would cook in her oven.

They walked through the house together in a light and airy silence. Sera looked around confused, worried that she didn't get the chance to shut the door before they were standing around her kitchen island. When her mind finally returned to him, Jacob gazed deeply into her eyes, leaned his chest over the table, and said–

"How've you been, Sera?" He said it quietly, but firmly. He said it like he'd said it a million times before.

"Oh, you know… it's been hard," Sera nodded along, "But I get by, yes." Still, that look never left his face, even as he smiled and clapped his hands together.

"Well, I am rubbish at cooking, but I swore I'd make an effort– and with such lovely company awaiting me, I should be able to pull something together well enough," he said, still carefully eyeing her.

She smiled, always so shy when she was with him. She would shield her face with her hand, hiding in her hair or her shoulder, never quite able to meet his eye for longer than a moment. Thus, she turned away from him.

Jacob's demeanor chilled just as Sera's eyes met the small, gilded clock that sat upon the windowsill above the sink. It read forty-five past seven. It always read forty-five past seven. Though Sera came and went, forty-six past seven never arrived. She felt a small ache in the back of her head. It grew larger and deeper until she felt that she couldn't see, couldn't breathe. A great, terrible scratching noise overhead only deepened her anxieties. Sera heard the familiar sound of the armoire in the guest bedroom being shoved across the floor. With tears in her eyes, she returned Jacob's gaze and smiled, her breath wheezing out of her in short bursts.

"What's on the menu tonight?"

The concern never left his eyes as he smiled, grabbed a few vegetables out of the bags he had brought, and said heartily, "Brisket."

She watched him quietly as he expertly diced and cut different vegetables and meats that she could not remember the name of. A steaming cup of tea sat before her that she lifted to her lips every so often. He grinned at her just as frequently. They spoke about trivial things, the mail carrier and his forgetfulness, Jacob's dog Bruno, Sera's work at the high school in town. It was nice. It was very pleasant.

"Do you think mother will make it home for dinner?" she asked.

Jacob looked up from his work and smiled at her, his eyes soft and swimming with her image as he responded, "I'm sure."

Though even as he said it, Sera was sure that he was wrong. This hasn't happened the way it was supposed to happen. "Wait--"

"Not sure that my cooking could ever satisfy the great Charlotte Jenkins, but she will no doubt be present and mocking me," he said with a soft laugh.

"No, this isn't right." Sera looked to Jacob and saw only his kind face as it fell into those same soft edges, as his lips rounded into a soft line.

"I know, dear."

Together, they shared a single moment of pure and dry lucidity before Sera laughed, banishing the shards of glass that cut through her mind.

"I'm– I'm sorry, I'm not quite sure what I… oh do forgive me," she said sweetly.

Jacob didn't move. He looked at her knowingly, painfully, before returning his gaze to the slab of meat before him.

"I… Jacob, what time is it?"

He didn't look up at her. The seven clocks in Jenkins Manor struck on the hour, but when Sera looked at the small clock above the sink, it still read forty-five past seven. Above her, she heard the sound of drills, of walls being torn away, drywall being knocked down. Sera looked up at the ceiling but returned to Jacob just as quickly.

"Oh, Jacob?"

"Sera," he said curtly, looking up at her as he set a large knife down on the counter. The tone of his voice cut through all efforts of Sera's imagination as he said, "why are we here?"

"I… I don't know what you mean, Jacob. We're… we're eating dinner."

"I haven't finished cooking yet," Jacob said, sitting across from her in the dining room. Those thin, black glasses that always decorated his face, fogged with the steam of freshly cooked beef.

The smell of carrots, celery, and meat filled the room.

"You're always coming back here," he said.

"Looks delicious," she said with a smile. Though she did not look down at her plate. She did not look towards the kitchen or its window. She did not look toward the great and ominous grandfather clock in the corner of the room. She looked only at Jacob as the edges of her vision began to fade; his face painted with a mere fraction of the pain and panic that plagued Sera's mind.

"Do you want to try again?"

"Hmm?" She wasn't sure what he meant, but just the same she heard a knock at the door.

"Hi there!" Sera had always liked Jacob. He lived just a few minutes down the street. He'd come over for something– "I was hoping I could borrow your oven." The way he spoke made her chest warm. His face danced with every word; his eyes always alight with fervor. "Mine's just busted, I'm afraid."

"Of course! Yes, please, come in." He was carrying bags, Sera realized. Probably full of whatever food he would cook in her oven.

They walked through the house together, in a light and airy silence. Sera looked around confused, worried that she didn't get the chance to shut the door before they found themselves standing around her kitchen island. When her mind finally returned to him, Jacob gazed deeply into her eyes, leaned his chest over the table, and said–

"How've you been, Sera?" He said it quietly, but firmly. He said it like he'd said it a million times before.

Sera meant to smile, but something scratched at her insides. "I'm sorry, have we done this before?"

Jacob sighed deeply and stepped backward. "Yes, Sera, we have." He set the knife down beside a pile of diced celery.

"W-why?" she asked with a laugh, but her mind flooded with trepidation, black and thick like tar. Dread stained her insides like smoke on cloth.

"You tell me," Jacob said, sitting across from her in the dining room. Those thin, black, glasses that always decorated his face, fogged with the steam of freshly cooked beef. The smell of carrots, celery, and meat filled the room.

"This happened months ago," she said.

He nodded, worry and pain still pouring out of him as he smiled at her, that same sad smile.

"Your first night back at the house in so many years."

"I never liked this place much."

"No, you didn't. So, you stayed away until Charlotte needed you."

"Mother…"

"We sat, we ate, and when your mother arrived home from her appointment," Jacob paused just long enough for Sera to hear the light knocking at the front door, "she joined us."

"Oh!" Sera exclaimed, tossing the napkin that laid in her lap onto the table. "That must be the nurse with mother! I'll get it."

"No, Sera." Jacob grabbed her wrist just as she began to rise from her chair. "This happened months ago."

"My first night back…"

"Yes." He released her.

She sat back in her chair, staring down at the dark, wooden countertop. She felt oddly like she was waking up. "I always liked this night."

"Why this one?"

"You were just so full of life. So full that I could feel it spilling out into the room and filling me up with that same… energy." She looked down at the floor like she could see it, all of his happiness and joy pooling at their feet. She reached out her hands like she could wet them in it, like she could wash her skin with it, like it might wipe away the rot. "I felt alive when I was with you."

Jacob looked on at her, kind but sad. He reached across the table and grabbed her hand.

"Are you ready this time?"

The clock struck on the hour, but there were no clocks to look at, no way to check the time down here. She recognized these dark walls and rickety stairs as the same ones that she climbed as a young girl when she would play down here. She was underneath the house, in the storm cellar. What possessed Charlotte to allow her to play in such a dark and secluded room, with no way to check on her, was beyond Sera; but oh, she loved those days in the cellar, playing house.

The air was sticky and eerily still. Her breath blew clouds into the air, but she couldn't feel the cold. Turning in a slow circle around the room, she spotted the same pair of shoes she always saw in the cellar. Brown, leather heeled boots, attached to dark stockings, lay just beyond the staircase.

"Hello?" called Sera. "Are you alright?"

Slowly, she approached, rounding the corner of the stairs. She had always loved those boots. She could wear them for hours without paining her toes.

"Hello?"

As she came into view, so did Sera. She saw it, felt it. The knot in her head, the stiffness of her neck, the blood in her eyes. She peered over the figure, and she saw herself. She saw her bloodied head resting against the concrete floor. She saw her shoulders, slumped so uncomfortably forward; her eyes glazed and stunned. Sera heard the familiar sound of soft, booted footsteps, the tapping of plastic as he folded his glasses; but she knew better than to turn around, knew better than to meet his eye when he found her. Sera hummed as she looked at the groceries beside her lifeless hand, they'd be no good now.

"Oh," was all she said as she heard the chiming of the clocks on the hour.

Turning on her heel and looking up at the stairs, she smiled. There was a knock at the door.

"Hi there!" Sera had always liked Jacob. He lived just a few minutes down the street. He'd come over for something– "I was hoping I could borrow your oven." The way he spoke made her chest warm. His face danced with every word; his eyes always alight with fervor. "Mine's just busted, I'm afraid."

"Of course! Yes, please, come in."

The Mirror

I was doing my makeup that morning when I got the call. I thought I might go shopping, grab some food. It was my only day off from work, and the long hours were endlessly draining. Order after order, two scoops of this, sixteen ounces of that, customer after customer, the banality of it, the repetition that characterizes the suburbs—I just wanted to feel like a person. I spent so little time taking care of myself back then. I hardly ate--just showered, slept, and went back to work, day in and day out. I was a ghost in my own home. For six days, I had not taken a step single step out of my house without that abhorrent uniform on. So, on the morning of my only day off, I made a point to spend the entire day doing whatever I wanted.

I was doing my makeup when I got the call.

Hey sweetie, what are you doing…well, I just called to tell you that… umm… Hunter's dead.

--

Time is a fickle and irritating thing. It's easy to be so concerned with the future when we are so convinced that it exists. People are needy, people are sick and tired and sad, and it is easier to imagine a straight line. A straight, little line, where they can draw dots at set points, and say, see, this is it, this is the past, I remember, it's there, it's real. But it's not. We are just two-dimensional dots, moving through three-dimensional space, observing life in instants, perceiving the change in distance as time. There's no going back. Our memories are the only evidence of past events, and our memories are just us. They exist only as we exist now, and like a reflection, our memories are flawed. They're inauthentic-- exaggerated or minimized, changed and altered past the point of recognition.

Are you okay? Aunt Kris wanted me to call everyone… I can't believe this is real.

Yeah… yeah, I'm okay.

Time is a fickle and irritating thing, but I escaped it in that moment. Silence consumed me and I spent an eternity staring at my mirror. My first thought was not of my cousin, but of my mascara. I had only done one eye. Should I do the other?

I think I might be a bad person.

We got off the phone and I finished my makeup.

--

There was something wrong with my reflection. The woman staring back at me was a carbon copy, down to the freckles on my cheeks, but she wasn't me. The person staring back at me was bored. She was painted and absent, like a mannequin. There was something disrespectful, something untoward about the way she just stood there, looking back at me. There was no sign of life, no sign of grief, no sign of the pressure in my chest that grew and grew. There was no sign of the waters raging inside me, the straining of my throat as they pulled me down and down and–

I'm not breathing. I don't think I'm breathing anymore. I can't breathe.

I struggled against the tide, but it took me. As my head rose above the water, I saw no hope of reprieve, no chance of survival as I sank back down. I was blinded and then gifted my sight, only to have it ripped from me once more. The water was cold, but my muscles burned with an effort greater than I had ever expended. It was quiet and then deafeningly loud. I was silent and then I was screaming. It almost seemed kinder below the waves. Again, these raging waters wrenched me up into the air; again, I looked as far as the horizon, and I saw nothing as I was dragged out in the undertow. Again, there was no land. Again, no clouds. Again, no hope. Again, it was just me there.

And her.

She didn't flinch as my lips became blue, as the veins in my eyes burst from the overwhelming pressure in my skull. She didn't reach out to me as I puked in the sink before us. Not a single muscle in her body moved as I lifted my head and screamed at her.

Who are you?

Staring back at me from beyond the glass was a separate entity. She would have looked pretty, if she were not so eerily still, not so disgustingly calm—she would have looked beautiful. It was almost blasphemous, the way her hair sat so perfectly on her shoulders– the absence of fly-aways. How could she stand there like that, so pretty and perfect, while I am drowning in front of her? How could she sit there, porcelain and absent, while my cousin lies dead?

She studied me just as I did her. It was all I could do to keep from succumbing to the apathy creeping up my spine. I shuddered and shivered against it until I finally forced it down, and I stared back. I let myself be angry. I let myself rage, unrestrained like those waters. I hated her for the bronzer on her cheek bones and the blush beneath her eyes. I hated her for her perfectly plucked brows, for her painted lashes. I hated her for having such soft, clean skin, while Hunter's lay rotting on a metal slab; being poked and prodded by a stranger who has poked and prodded so many other dead bodies, like that's all my cousin was, just another corpse in a long string of autopsies and grieving families. I hated her for the way she mocked me, just a two-dimensional dot, on a three-dimensional plane, forced to keep moving forward while she remained. I hated her for the way time abandoned her while I could not stop the world from moving on. It should have stopped. The world should have stopped. I hated her for the pause that I was not allowed.

My fist trickled with blood as I lowered it back onto the counter. She was gone. All that remained of her decorated the countertop in glass shards, and instead of staring at that girl, I stared at the wall. I stared deep into the drywall, tried to shove my consciousness somewhere in between the support beams behind it. I wanted to climb inside the wall and live out the rest of my life somewhere that time could not get to me. I wanted to live inside that instant. Away from the woman in my shattered mirror, away from the waves, away from any present moment without Hunter in it.

Honey? Are you there? Can you get a hold of your mom for me? I've been trying to call her but she's not picking up. I don't want you to have to tell her.

Yeah, I'll call her.

We said our I love you's before we said our goodbyes, because we both had a renewed sense of time and its fickleness.

We got off the phone and my first thought was of my mascara.

A single tear rolled down my cheek as I grabbed a wet rag and dragged it across my face.

I had only done one eye.

The Cemetery

While a loving husband, Mr. Covington is still an old, working man. His skeleton heavy with weight and thick with scars from a life that seems so long ago as he cements the walls of this house brick after brick. He wipes the sweat from his brow with a quick flick of his leathered hands, just the backs of them, to keep from scratching his face on his calloused palms. If one only looks, they might see him sink to his knees as he starts each row of cemented brick. And just the same, one might watch him slowly rise to his feet as the walls grow tall and sturdy. You might see him looking on into the garden, to his wife, as he leans in the plush grass to build the walls of their bedroom. She is tall and soft and careful as she plants dianthus and delphiniums down into the soil—as if to bring life to the surrounding oak and pine. He watches her, just as we all do, as she looks up to the sky, lifting her face to meet the warm summer sun—capturing the heat in all its comfort. And it is with that image in mind that he decides to put in so many windows-- long and narrow windows that point so perfectly to the east-- so that every morning she may be greeted with the same warmth that washes her in such solace.

Some mornings one might peer into their kitchen, pondering the ledge over the sink—under a window with white, wooden shutters. The old man's wife will be putting her leftover scallions into glass jars full of water and placing them on the windowsill. The old man will leave his freshly washed dishes on a drying rack on the ledge; he was never the type to own a dishwasher, not when he knew he could get the job done by hand. Other mornings you might find the pair with their children. At times they are young and jubilant, running through the gardens as a tired Mr. Covington cuts tomatoes off the vine. Other times they are older, angrier. Very rarely, you will find an unfamiliar adult standing over a patch of freshly upturned soil, crying. The child hadn't been home for quite some time. She hadn't known that she was sick. Mostly, you will see Mr. Covington tending to his garden and holding his wife. They are such a happy couple.

One might think that, in his youth, Mr. Covington never thought he'd live in a house with a windowsill over the sink in the kitchen. Maybe he'd never thought to wonder how best to bring nature and sunlight indoors in such a pleasing manner, as he did for his dear and darling wife. Perhaps he never believed he would've met a woman so wonderful that he'd think it a blessing to be able to wonder such a thing. Maybe he'd never wanted to impress someone so badly. One would imagine that old Mr. Covington never thought he'd dig her a grave; he must never have imagined carving her a head stone. One might say that absolutely he could not have thought he'd lay her so gently to rest. Still, all of this is speculation. One can only guess about the bodies that lie in Covington's cemetery. One can only guess about their lives since they have been lost and forgotten.

Still, there are few things of which we are all certain. Certainly, every morning that they rise from their plots, Mr. and Mrs. Covington love each other-- and it is certain because every moment that they spend above their sullen graves, they cling to each other. And certainly-- painfully, the way that it is so certain-- Mr. Covington is distraught. Every second that his eyes spend departed from his love, he looks out onto the cemetery he once called home, the land he once laid his wife to rest in, and he is devastated beyond doubt. His eyes swim with the ghost of what his home had once been. During his short bursts of lucidity, you might see him plod up to the walls on the far end of the Cemetery and weep for his friends that have been lost to pavement and lease agreements. Sometimes you will hear him send thanks to the heavens that have denied him. He extends his gratitude to an absent god for the mere fact that the bodies of his wife and neighbors have yet to be paved over and built upon. Sometimes he sits near his wife and stares off at the ragged and freezing homeless that clean the grounds in thanks for a place to rest their weary heads. Mr. Covington sends his thanks to them as well. Sometimes, he will smile and watch as students from a local school cutaway fallen tree branches and remove the limbs. Sometimes he will smile and shake the hands of the nameless, whose graves were not marked, showing them kindness, and offering refuge from the dark, liminal space they all inhabit when they are not haunting the grounds.

One might think that Mr. Covington, that old, working man, will spend the rest of eternity tending that old, forgotten cemetery. To that, Mr. Covington would say, at least Mrs. Covington is with him.

To Milinda Stephenson

Thank you for every comment made, every point taken, and every

tear I shed while looking at my graded papers. I could not have

gotten here without your guiding hands.

Made in the USA
Monee, IL
25 July 2022